Wempires

written and illustrated by

DANIEL PINKWATER

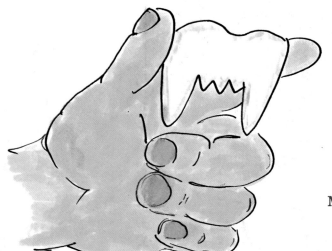

Macmillan Publishing Company   New York
Maxwell Macmillan Canada   Toronto
Maxwell Macmillan International Publishing Group
New York   Oxford   Singapore   Sydney

Macmillan Publishing Company
866 Third Avenue
New York, NY 10022

Maxwell Macmillan Canada, Inc.
1200 Eglinton Avenue East
Suite 200
Don Mills, Ontario M3C 3N1
Macmillan Publishing Company is part of the Maxwell
Communication Group of Companies.
First edition
Printed in Singapore
10   9   8   7   6   5   4   3   2   1
The text of this book is set in 14 pt. ITC Cushing Medium.
The illustrations are rendered in pen and ink with color markers.
Book design by Christy Hale

Library of Congress Cataloging-in-Publication Data
Pinkwater, Daniel Manus.
Wempires / written and illustrated by Daniel Pinkwater. — 1st ed.
       p.   cm.
Summary: At the height of his vampire craze, Jonathan meets some
real vampires and finds they are not quite what he expected.
ISBN 0-02-774411-6
[1. Vampires—Fiction.] I. Title.
PZ7.P6335We   1991
[E]—dc   20 90-46925

To F. W. Murnau

I saw a movie on TV one Saturday afternoon. It was about a vampire. What a good movie!

The vampire was scary. He was real smooth. I liked his clothes.

I decided I would be a vampire.

I asked my mother to help me make a
vampire costume.
"But Halloween was three months ago,"
she said.
"Just the same," I said, "I'd like you to
help me make the costume. Please."
Actually, she made the whole thing.
It was very good.

I smeared my face with white stuff my mother uses at night, and I rubbed my hair with salad oil so it would be shiny and smooth. I used a little red lipstick. I looked good.

Then I waited in the hallway for my sister to come by. It is fairly dark in the hallway.

It was a big success.

I turned up at supper in my vampire suit. Everybody thought it was cute. My father took pictures. Every time I looked at my sister she burst into tears.

I practiced doing vampire moves and saying vampire things.

The first problem came the next morning. They wouldn't let me wear my vampire suit to school.

"None of the other children go around wearing capes," my mother
said.

"That's because they don't have any," I said.

"Look, you can't go to school dressed like a vampire."

"Why not?"

"Because I am your mother, and I say you can't. You may put on your
vampire suit when you come home."

"Could I sleep in a coffin, do you think?" I asked.
"This is getting weird," my mother said.

After school, I went to the dime store and got the one thing I really needed—fake plastic vampire teeth.

The next day my teacher sent a note home with me.

Dear Mrs. Harker,

Jonathan has been threatening to bite children in his class. I have asked him to leave his fangs at home. I hope you will have a little talk with him.

Yours truly,

Mildred Van Helsing

Mildred Van Helsing (Teacher)

My parents had a little talk with me. They said that they thought I would get tired of being a vampire. They said I could wear my cape and fangs and things around the house—but I was not to dress or act like a vampire at school.

I'll never get tired of being a vampire, I thought.

My parents also said that if I didn't cooperate, they would take steps.

"What steps would you take?" I asked them.

"Steps," they said. "Just go to your room and think about it."

I went to my room and cut out bats. I hung them from the ceiling on pieces of thread. They looked pretty good.

That night, when I was sleeping, vampires came through the window. I woke up.

"Hallo, sonnyboy!" the vampires said. "How's by you?"

"Wait a minute!" I said. "Are you guys vampires?"

"Wempires! That's us!" the vampires said.

"Real ones?"

"Of course real! What did you think, fake wempires?"

"And you can turn into bats?"

"Any time we like."

"And you …uh …drink people's blood?"

"Fooey! What a disgusting idea! Where did you hear that?"

"Everybody knows that," I said.

"Fooey! From television you get such ideas. Drinking blood—yich!" said the vampires. "Now for drinking, ginger ale is best. Maybe you have some ginger ale in the house?"

"There might be some in the icebox," I said.

"And chicken. Chicken we eat."

"There might be some cold chicken, too."

"Cold chicken is good. Let's go down to the kitchen, sonnyboy. Don't make noise and wake up the family."

The vampires followed me down the stairs to the kitchen.

There was most of a cooked chicken in the icebox, and the vampires found two family-size bottles of ginger ale. They ate the chicken, and drank a lot of ginger ale. Then they burped.

"Hey, sonnyboy! Do you got any onions?" they asked. They opened cans of sardines, toasted slices of whole wheat bread, and made sardine and onion sandwiches. When they had finished those, they poured corn flakes into bowls, and sloshed milk over them.

The vampires were making a mess of the kitchen. They were having a good time. They sang a song.

"Sing the song with us, sonnyboy!" the vampires said.

I don't care for peaches. They are full of stones.
I like bananas because they have no bones.

All of a sudden, my mother was standing in the doorway. She was wearing her bathrobe. "What's this? Vampires in my kitchen in the middle of the night?"

"Hallo, sonnyboy's mother," the
vampires said.

"There are crumbs everywhere," my
mother said.

"We having a party," the vampires said.

"Out," my mother said.

"Out?" asked the vampires.

"Out now," my mother said.

"Well, good-bye, sonnyboy," the vampires said. They climbed out the kitchen window.

"I didn't know they would mess up the kitchen," I said.

"Now do you see why your father and I didn't want you to behave like a vampire?" my mother said.

"They didn't mean any harm," I said.

"Go to your room."

I went to my room. I looked out my window. The vampires were making their way down the street. They waved to me. "Good-bye, sonnyboy!
Be a good wempire!"

What neat guys! Nothing will ever change my mind about being a
vampire.